WIGGLESBOTTOM PRIMARY
THE CLASSROOM CAT

PAMELA BUTCHART

BECKA MOOR

nosy crow

SUSIE

MR HARRIS

SUNITA

ROZ

GAVIN

JOEL

ANNE-MARIE

BOBBY

THEO

First published in 2019 by Nosy Crow Ltd
The Crow's Nest, 14 Baden Place,
Crosby Row, London SE1 1YW

www.nosycrow.com

ISBN: 978 1 78800 122 9

Nosy Crow and associated logos are trademarks and/or registered
trademarks of Nosy Crow Ltd

A CIP catalogue record for this book is available from the British Library.

Printed in China.

Papers used by Nosy Crow are made
from wood grown in
sustainable forests.

5 7 9 8 6 4

CONTENTS

The first time we saw the Classroom Cat was on a Monday.

We were all in a bit of a **BAD MOOD** because on Mondays the dinner ladies serve **THE FISH** for dinners and we all hate

THE FISH.

But then Evie McIntosh gasped and pointed to Miss Riley's desk and said,

"LOOK!"

So we all looked and that's when we saw the **BIGGEST** and **MOST STRIPY** cat we had **EVER** seen.

The cat was sitting **RIGHT** on top of Miss Riley's keyboard and none of us knew what to do so we all just **STARED** at him.

But then Miss Riley walked into the classroom and saw the cat and she

SCREAMED

and he jumped out of the window and disappeared.

Everyone was talking about the Classroom Cat and how he had been sitting on Miss Riley's keyboard and how **STRIPY** he was and how Miss Riley wouldn't let us open the windows even though it was **REALLY** hot because she was scared he might come back.

But then Jayden King gasped and said, **"LOOK!"**

And that's when we saw that the Classroom

Cat **WAS BACK**. He was sitting on a tree branch outside the window beside Miss Riley's desk and he was **STARING**

8

at her as she typed on her keyboard.

That's when Irfan Baxter said, "I think he was sitting on the keyboard for **A REASON**."

But we didn't know what **THE REASON** was so we asked Irfan if he knew and he took a deep breath and said, **"YES"** and we all **GASPED**.

That's when Irfan said that cats can't talk but that maybe the Classroom Cat was trying to **COMMUNICATE** with us using Miss Riley's keyboard and that that was why he'd been sitting on it.

We had **NO IDEA** what the Classroom Cat needed to tell us but we could all tell by how much he was **STARING** at Miss Riley that it was **SERIOUS**.

So we waited until Miss Riley left her desk and then Megan McNally rushed over and opened the window and sat back down before Miss Riley could see her.

And that's when we knew for a **FACT** that Irfan had been right about the **URGENT MESSAGE** because the Classroom Cat **LEAPT** through the window and on to Miss Riley's keyboard as soon as Megan opened the window.

We all watched as the Classroom Cat walked over the keyboard and then he must have pressed **PRINT** because the printer started making a noise and the Classroom

Cat jumped back out the window. And we all **GASPED** because the Classroom Cat had obviously typed us a message.

Evie McIntosh rushed over to the printer and brought back a piece of paper and it said:

WURGLEFSSSSHHHH

But none of us knew what **"WURGLEFSSSSHHHH"** meant.

So Irfan Baxter ran to get a

DICTIONARY.

But **"WURGLEFSSSSHHHH"** wasn't in it.

Irfan said that it was because the dictionary

only has **HUMAN WORDS** in it and that we were obviously going to need a

CAT
DICTIONARY.

As soon as the bell went for break we all **RAN** to the library and asked the librarian for a **CAT DICTIONARY** and she gave us a book called "A-Z of Cats" but we couldn't find the word **"WURGLEFSSSSHHHH"** in it **ANYWHERE**.

And then all of a sudden we heard **TAPPING** and we looked up and saw the Classroom Cat was **BACK** and that he was tapping at the window with his paw!

So we all ran over and opened the window and the Classroom Cat crawled in and started walking along a row of bookshelves **REALLY SLOWLY**.

Irfan said that the Classroom Cat obviously wanted us to follow him. So we did. And we kept following him until he eventually stopped next to a **COOKBOOK**.

We watched closely as the Classroom Cat sniffed at the book and then he placed his paw **RIGHT** on top of it and turned and

STARED at us with **WIDE EYES**.

We all knew that the Classroom Cat was trying to tell us something and that it must be something to do with the **COOKBOOK** and that it was **IMPORTANT** but we **STILL** didn't know what it was.

But then all of a sudden the end-of-break bell went and the Year 1s came rushing into the library and the Classroom Cat jumped out the window again.

When we were walking to school dinners we heard a **WEIRD CHATTERING SOUND** and we looked and saw that it was the **CLASSROOM CAT**.

He was opening and shutting his mouth **LOADS** and making **WEIRD SOUNDS** through the glass.

Irfan Baxter said that it was obviously a **WARNING CRY** and that the Classroom Cat was **FOLLOWING US** and that danger must be **NEAR**.

And that's when Evie McIntosh said, "**OH NO!** I know what the

DANGER

isl I think he's trying to warn us about

And we all knew that Evie McIntosh was **RIGHT** because the Classroom Cat had put his paw on a **COOKBOOK** in the library and **STARED** at us (and also because **THE FISH** was **DISGUSTING**).

That's when Irfan **GASPED** and he said, **"SHOW ME THE PAPER!"**

So I held up the piece of paper that the Classroom Cat had printed out for us.

Irfan pointed to the word and said, **"LOOK!** It says

"WURGLE" and then "FSSSSHHHH".

He was trying to write

FISH!"

Irfan said that he couldn't be one hundred per cent sure but that he was **NINETY-NINE PER CENT** sure that "WURGLE" meant "DANGEROUS" in cat language and that none of us should touch the

DANGEROUS FISH.

Not even with our **HANDS** in case it melted our skin off.

So we didn't. We all just went up to the hot counter with our trays and took the **DANGEROUS FISH** and sat back down and **STARED AT IT**.

But then all of a sudden the Classroom Cat

rushed **RIGHT ACROSS** the dining hall and jumped up on to our table and started eating Jayden King's dangerous fish.

That's when Jayden yelled, "Look! He's trying to **PROTECT ME!**"

And Jayden was right because as soon as the Classroom Cat finished he started eating Megan McNally's fish, too!

Irfan Baxter said that **THE FISH** must just be dangerous to **HUMANS** and that cats must be **IMMUNE** to it which means that they can't catch a disease from it like we can.

We all watched as the Classroom Cat finished everyone's dangerous fish in less than **ONE MINUTE** and then he just sat in the middle of the table next to the water jug, licking himself.

So that's when we all started clapping because the Classroom Cat was obviously a hero and he had just saved our lives!

But then one of the dinner ladies came rushing over to see what we were clapping about and when she saw the Classroom Cat she started **SHOOING** him away because she obviously didn't know who he was.

So we tried to explain about the **DANGEROUS FISH** but that just made her more annoyed and then she ran off to get Mr Harris, the head teacher.

Mr Harris got a bit of a shock when he arrived and saw the Classroom Cat because the Classroom Cat had his head in the water jug and also because Mr Harris probably wasn't expecting to see a **HERO CAT** at our school that day.

Mr Harris reached over the table and tried to pick the Classroom Cat up but the Classroom Cat leapt off the table and ran across the dining room and out into the playground before anyone could stop him.

That's when Mr Harris told us that **THE FISH** definitely **WASN'T**

DANGEROUS and that the Classroom Cat **WASN'T** trying to warn us about it. And that he'd been trying to get into the school all day because he smelled the fish and cats like fish.

But then the dinner ladies gave Mr Harris a plate of **THE FISH** and Mr Harris looked at it and got a **WEIRD LOOK** on his face.

And we all knew that he believed us now about the **DANGEROUS FISH** and that he was wishing he hadn't made the Classroom Cat leave because he obviously needed his help!

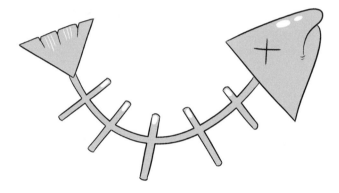

THE PUDDLE CRISP

One time at break Bobby Henderson dropped his last crisp in a puddle and everyone started chanting

  "Eat **IT**! Eat **IT**! Eat **IT**!"

  And he did.

We were all shocked because that's just something we say sometimes when someone drops their snack on the ground and no one actually thought he would do it.

Susie Keys said that we shouldn't have done the **CHANTING THING** because she was worried that Bobby Henderson might have a

SERIOUS DISEASE

now because you are not supposed to drink from puddles and you are definitely not supposed to dip crisps in them.

So we all asked Bobby if he felt **OK** and also why he did it.

Bobby said that he was feeling fine and that he wasn't sure why he'd eaten the **PUDDLE CRISP** and that he just thought it would be funny.

That's when some of the Year 6s came over

and they said that Susie Keys was **RIGHT** and that Bobby Henderson was definitely going to get

PUDDLE-POX.

We had **NO IDEA** what **PUDDLE-POX** was so we asked one of the Year 6s and they said that it was the same as

THE PLAGUE but **WORSE**.

Irfan Baxter **GASPED** because he'd read about **THE PLAGUE** before and people got **ANGRY SPOTS** all over their

bodies and they were really **ITCHY** and **RED**. But **PUDDLE-POX** was **EVEN WORSE!**

Bobby got a **WEIRD LOOK** on his

face and said that he wasn't feeling very
well all of a sudden and we all

GASPED

because we knew that Bobby was going to get the **ANGRY SPOTS!**

So we all **RAN** to the school nurse and told her about the **CRISP** and the **PUDDLE** and the **PUDDLE-POX**. But the nurse said that there was **NO SUCH THING** as **PUDDLE-POX** and that we definitely shouldn't eat any more crisps out of puddles because we might get upset stomachs.

But then at lunch Bobby said that his arm felt hot and that it was **TINGLING** a bit.

And then he rolled up his sleeve and we all saw that he had

THREE ANGRY SPOTS

on his arm!

Susie Keys said that it was **ONLY A MATTER OF TIME** before Bobby's **WHOLE BODY** was covered in angry spots and that the nurse must have been wrong about **PUDDLE-POX** not existing.

And she said that **PUDDLE-POX** was probably just such a **RARE DISEASE** that some school nurses didn't know about it. And that made sense.

Bobby said that he was starting to feel a bit hot so we all gave him the rest of our ice cream to try to cool him down which was a really nice thing for us all to do because it was **STRAWBERRY** ice cream with **ACTUAL REAL**

STRAWBERRIES in it.

As soon as Bobby had finished all the strawberry ice cream, we asked him if he was feeling any better but he said that he wasn't and that he was feeling **WORSE**.

That's when Susie Keys said that we must find a **CURE** before it was **TOO LATE**. So we went outside and asked the Year 6s about a cure and they said that they would tell us if David Barry let them play with his football for a **WHOLE DAY** because David Barry has a fancy, professional football that he won't let anyone touch without his permission.

So we all looked at David Barry. But he just looked at the ground. So Susie Keys grabbed Bobby's arm and rolled up his sleeve and stuck his red, blotchy arm **RIGHT** next to David Barry's face so he could see how bad it was and David Barry said, "**OK**."

Susie Keys took the football out of David Barry's hand and gave it to one of the Year

6s. And **THAT'S** when they told us that the **ONLY CURE** for **PUDDLE-POX** was to cover your **WHOLE BODY** in puddle water.

So we all **RUSHED** back over to the puddle where Bobby had dropped his crisp and eaten it and started splashing puddle water on him.

But then Bobby said that it **WASN'T WORKING** and he was

SUPER ITCHY

now and we could see that his skin had gone all red and blotchy.

That's when Irfan Baxter said that Bobby needed to **LIE DOWN** in the puddle and **ROLL AROUND** in it.

So he did and Susie said that we should splash water on him too, to be helpful.

And that's when our teacher, Miss Riley, came rushing over and she made us all stop splashing the puddle water on to Bobby.

And then she made him stand up and
EXPLAIN HIMSELF.

But Bobby was **TOO ITCHY** so we
explained for him. And that's when Miss
Riley said that **PUDDLE-POX** wasn't
real.

Miss Riley looked closely at Bobby's skin and asked him if he'd ever had **CHICKENPOX** when he was little. And Bobby said he hadn't.

So Miss Riley said he should go home and put some pink stuff on his **CHICKENPOX** and that the Year 6s were just pretending about the **PUDDLE-POX**.

We looked over and saw that some of the Year 6s were laughing and pointing at us.

So Miss Riley shouted,

"COME HERE, PLEASE!"

And the Year 6s stopped laughing and came over. But then one of them dropped David Barry's football and it fell **RIGHT** into the

puddle and splashed all the Year 6s and
they ran away **SCREAMING**.

And we shouted, "Mind you don't get

PUDDLE-POX!" And we

LAUGHED!

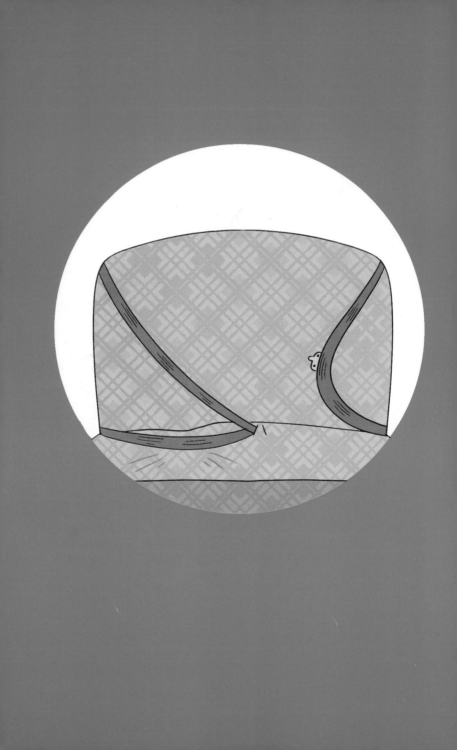

One time on our school trip to the museum, Lauren Carr tried to sit next to Joel Jack on the bus but Joel Jack yelled, "Don't sit there! Margaret's sitting there!"

We were all a bit confused because we do not **HAVE** someone in our class called **MARGARET** and also because the seat next to Joel Jack was completely **EMPTY**.

Theo Burke **GASPED** and said that Margaret was probably a **BUS GHOST** and that if you sat on her she would haunt you for **LIFE**. And that's when Lauren Carr said that she **DEFINITELY** didn't want to get haunted so she went and found another seat.

But Joel said that Margaret wasn't a **BUS GHOST** and that she was his

IMAGINARY FRIEND

and that he'd had her since he was a baby and that **MARGARET** really liked museums so he'd brought her along on the school trip.

None of us were really sure that we believed Joel about his **IMAGINARY FRIEND** but then loads of

WEIRD STUFF

started to happen on the bus. Like when Miles McKay's can of juice **EXPLODED**.

And when the bottom of the plastic bag **BUS BIN** ripped and all the rubbish went rolling down the aisle.

And when Susie Keys lost her coat for **AGES** until she eventually found it under a seat **FOUR ROWS** in front of where she was sitting!

And even though we couldn't prove it we thought that **MARGARET** might have something to do with it all.

So we turned around in our seats and asked Joel if Margaret was **REAL** or not and we made sure to whisper in case she **WAS** real. And that's when Joel said that Margaret was

ONE HUNDRED PER CENT REAL

and also that there was **NO NEED** to whisper because Margaret had gone to **STRETCH HER LEGS**.

And we all

GASPED

because we had **NO IDEA** where Margaret was **STRETCHING HER LEGS** and we were all worried that we might accidentally bang into her or trip over one of her legs or something.

Sunita Ram asked Joel Jack about Miles McKay's can of **EXPLODING JUICE** and the **ROLLING RUBBISH** and the coat that had **MOVED BY ITSELF**. And Joel Jack shook his head and started laughing and said, "Yup! That sounds like Margaret all right! She's always been a bit of a **PRANKSTER**."

And we all **GASPED** again because not only was imaginary Margaret

REAL

but we knew that she was a

PRANKSTER.

When we got to the **MUSEUM** Miss Riley made us all promise that we would be on our **BEST BEHAVIOUR** and she looked **RIGHT** at Joel Jack when she said it and Sunita said that it must be because Miss Riley **KNEW** about **IMAGINARY**

MARGARET.

Then when we got to the first **EXHIBITION** Joel Jack dropped his crisps **ALL OVER** the floor (even though we were definitely **NOT ALLOWED** to be

eating crisps inside the museum) and when
Miss Riley asked him to pick them up Joel

said, "It wasn't me! It was **MARGARET!**
She knocked them out of my hand!"

But Miss Riley made Joel pick them up
anyway and we all knew that it was probably
because she knew Imaginary Margaret's
fingers were made of **AIR** and that they

wouldn't be very good at picking up crisps.

Then when we all had a **TOILET BREAK** Jayden King came **RUNNING** out of the toilets and said that someone had chucked loads of **LOO ROLL** over the top of the cubicle when he was sitting on the toilet and that it had been so much that he

was sure it must have been a **FULL ROLL**.

Joel Jack turned and looked at the air next to him and started shaking his head backwards and forwards and saying, "Oh Margaret. You **KNOW** you're not allowed

in the boys' toilets!"

When we got to the very last **EXHIBITION** about **SHIPS** there was a sign up that said the exhibition was "**CLOSED**" and another sign that said

"WET PAINT"

so Miss Riley told us it was time to go to the

GIFT SHOP

and we all **CHEERED** because we'd been waiting to go to the gift shop since we got there!

But then all of a sudden one of the **MUSEUM PEOPLE** came rushing over and said, "That young man just touched the

wet paint!" and we looked and saw he was

pointing to Joel Jack
and also that there were
two hand prints on the
side of the **SHIP**.

But Joel Jack shook his head and said, "It wasn't me. It was **MARGARET!**"

So Miss Riley said, "Show me your hands."

But Joel Jack said that he **COULDN'T** show her his hands because Margaret had

them together and that she was

OUT OF CONTROL.

We all **GASPED** and shoved our hands in our pockets because we didn't want Margaret to superglue them.

Miss Riley stood there **STARING** at

Joel Jack and Joel Jack was **STARING BACK** and it looked a bit like they were having a **STARING COMPETITION**.

And then eventually Miss Riley said, "Joel. If you don't show me your hands then you won't be allowed to come on the next class trip."

We all felt bad for Joel because we knew that he **COULDN'T** show Miss Riley his hands because of the **SUPERGLUE** and that Miss Riley was being a bit unfair.

So that's when we explained about **MARGARET** and the **EXPLODING JUICE** and the **ROLLING RUBBISH** and the coat that **MOVED BY ITSELF**.

But Miss Riley said that David Barry's can of juice exploded because he'd been **SHAKING IT** before he got on the bus. And that the plastic bag **BUS BIN** had burst because we'd all brought far too many **BUS SNACKS**. And that Susie Keys had moved seats **FIVE TIMES** when she first got on the bus because she didn't like the way the seats **SMELLED** and that she must have forgotten to take her jacket with her one time.

So we all looked at Joel and he opened his hands and we all

GASPED

because the palms of his hands were covered in **ORANGE PAINT**.

And that's when we found out that **JOEL** had been making everything up and that there **WASN'T** a real imaginary person called Margaret.

Miss Riley made Joel sit on the bus while we went to the gift shop and when we got back to the bus Joel looked really upset. We

all thought that Joel was upset because he didn't get to go to the gift shop. But when we asked him he said that it **WASN'T** that. He was upset because Margaret had

DISAPPEARED.

So Sunita Ram took Joel Jack's hand and said that it was time to stop **TELLING TALES** and to **MOVE ON** and that Margaret hadn't actually been real anyway because he'd made her up.

But then all of a sudden Miss Riley

SQUEALED

and we looked up and saw that she had just opened a can of juice and that it had

EXPLODED

all over her!

And that's when Joel Jack looked at the empty seat next to him and said, "Welcome back, Margaret!"

And then he **HIGH-FIVED** the air and

we all

GASPED.

Also by PAMELA BUTCHART and
illustrated by BECKA MOOR

WIGGLESBOTTOM
PRIMARY
SuPER
DOG

PTO for a
SNEAK PEEK!

One time, a **DOG** got into the playground at morning break.

At first, we all thought it was a **WOLF** because it was **HUGE**. But Megan McNally said that it was **DEFINITELY NOT** a wolf because wolves are **WILD** so they don't wear collars.

The dog ran around the playground for ages and everyone **SCREAMED** whenever it came near them. But then Mr Harris, the deputy head, came out to see what all the **SCREAMING** was about and the dog disappeared.

EVERYONE was talking about the Playground Dog when we went back to the classroom and NO ONE could concentrate on their French like Miss Riley wanted us to do because we were all thinking about the dog.

Then Bobby Henderson gasped and pointed out of the window and shouted,

"HE'S BACK!"

But by the time we all got out of our seats and ran up to the window to see, Playground Dog had **DISAPPEARED** again.

Irfan Baxter said that it was a bit **WEIRD** how **BOTH TIMES** the dog had disappeared so quickly and that maybe Playground Dog had

POWERS.

That's when we all realised that this was

NO ORDINARY DOG.

At lunchtime, loads of people spotted Playground Dog in weird places and Megan McNally even thought she spotted his tail on the **ROOF**!

That's when Irfan said, "I can't believe it. **THAT'S** how he keeps disappearing. Playground Dog can **FLY!**"

Then Susie Keys shouted, "He's a **SUPER DOG!**"

And everyone gasped and someone started clapping. And then **EVERYONE** started clapping and shouting, **"SU-PER DOG! SU-PER DOG!"**

EVERYONE wanted to meet Super Dog but we didn't know what to do to stop him from flying away from us.

So that's when Susie Keys said that she would **SACRIFICE** her lunch so we could all meet Super Dog.

I didn't really know what that meant until Susie Keys took her cheese sandwich out of her lunch box and shouted,

"HEEEERE,
SUPER DOG!
YUMMY-YUMMY!"

Nothing happened for a bit. But then all of a sudden we heard a rustling sound and Super Dog came running out of the bushes and everyone

GASPED!

Susie Keys threw the cheese sandwich up in the air and Super Dog jumped up really high and caught it in his mouth and everyone

CHEERED!

We all stood in a circle around Super
Dog and watched while he ate the cheese
sandwich.

Once he was finished eating he sat down
and **STARED** at Megan McNally.

That's when Megan said her **EYES** felt weird and that she thought Super Dog was trying to **COMMUNICATE** with her through his **EYES**.

So Megan put out her hand and Super Dog licked her hand four times and then ran away.